Streaker, the hurricane ... is lost – help!

She really has to get back home to see Trevor (he'll be missing her) . . .

AND, most important of all, her puppies!

Jeremy Strong once worked in a bakery, putting the jam into three thousand doughnuts every night. Now he puts the jam in stories instead, which he finds much more exciting. At the age of three, he fell out of a first-floor bedroom window and landed on his head. His mother says that this damaged him for the rest of his life and refuses to take any responsibility. He loves writing stories because he says it is 'the only time you alone have complete control and can make anything happen'. His ambition is to make you laugh (or at least snuffle). Jeremy Strong lives near Bath with three cats and a flying cow.

Read more about Streaker's adventures

THE HUNDRED-MILE-AN-HOUR DOG
RETURN OF THE HUNDRED-MILE-AN-HOUR DOG
WANTED! THE HUNDRED-MILE-AN-HOUR DOG

Are you feeling silly enough to read more?

MY DAD'S GOT AN ALLIGATOR!
MY GRANNY'S GREAT ESCAPE
MY MUM'S GOING TO EXPLODE!
MY BROTHER'S FAMOUS BOTTOM
MY BROTHER'S FAMOUS BOTTOM GETS PINCHED

BEWARE! KILLER TOMATOES
CHICKEN SCHOOL

KRAZY KOW SAVES THE WORLD – WELL, ALMOST

Jeremy Strong

LOST!
The Hundred-Mile-An-Hour Dog

Illustrated by Rowan Clifford

PUFFIN

This is for Dazzy Donut lovers everywhere.

May the power be with you, whether you

have two legs or four.

PUFFIN BOOKS

Published by the Penguin Group
Penguin Books Ltd, 80 Strand, London WC2R 0RL, England
Penguin Group (USA) Inc., 375 Hudson Street, New York, New York 10014, USA
Penguin Group (Canada), 90 Eglinton Avenue East, Suite 700, Toronto, Ontario, Canada M4P 2Y3
Pen   ks Ltd)
P   tralia

Penguin   017, India
                                                                                            nd

Penguin F   South Africa
                                                                                            nd

The moral right of the author and illustrator has been asserted

Set in Baskerville MT
Made and printed in England by Clays Ltd, St Ives plc

British Library Cataloguing in Publication Data
A CIP catalogue record for this book is available from the British Library

ISBN: 978-0-141-32325-1

www.greenpenguin.co.uk

Mixed Sources
Product group from well-managed
forests and other controlled sources
www.fsc.org Cert no. SA-COC-1592
© 1996 Forest Stewardship Council

Penguin Books is committed to a sustainable future
for our business, our readers and our planet.
The book in your hands is made from paper
certified by the Forest Stewardship Council.

Contents

1 Pies!

It wasn't my fault. All I did was jump in the back of a van. What's wrong with that? In fact I was being really helpful. Trevor Two-Legs – the boy who is supposed to look after me – had gone wandering off. He's always doing that and then he gets lost. He should be kept on a lead. Trevor's hopeless when he's lost and he starts calling for me. 'Streaker? STREAKER!' What am I supposed to do? I KNOW WHERE I AM. HE'S THE ONE THAT'S LOST!

Anyhow, Trevor had disappeared as usual, leaving me all on my own. I was trotting about sniff-sniffing and there was this van with the back doors open, so I had a peep inside and guess what? It was full of pies and sausage rolls. It was!

A whole van full of pies and rolls. My favourite!

And I was thinking: *Hmmm, fancy leaving all those pies lying about like that. Someone could easily come along and steal the whole lot.*

The thing is, I've always fancied being a super-clever-guard-dog type of dog, only I've never been given the chance. I'd be an extra-super-special guard dog and I'd probably have super-powers too, and an extra-special name. I'd call myself DAZZY DONUT DOG.

That's DAZZY because Dazzy is a super-special word, and DONUT because Dazzy Donut Dog likes eating donuts. (Of course, really it's me – I like donuts. A WHOLE LOT.) And it's DOG because I'm a dog.

Dazzy Donut Dog lives in my head, where nobody can see her, except me. She has amazing super-special-powers, which she gets from eating SUPER-SPECIAL-POWER DAZZY DONUTS, with jam inside, or icing on the top. I keep all the donuts in my head too, but it's a BIG SECRET, so don't tell anyone.

Whenever there's trouble all I have to do is eat one of the super-special-power-donuts and KER-CHING!! I become Dazzy Donut Dog and go Whizz! Whoosh! Grrrrrr! Gotcha!

But that Trevor, he's useless. He never gives me anything to guard. I'm not complaining, because I like Trevor and his mum and dad. It's just that they're all a bit useless, being two-legs. Fancy having only two legs! That's a bit naff, isn't it?

I've never been given the chance to show them what I can really do. I could be the best guard dog ever, and if a robber came along I'd leap out and bark furiously and jump up and down – *boing-wuff! boing-wuff!* – like that. And if they came too close I'd dive at their ankles and bite them, *raargh-raargh, crunch-crunch!* like that. And they'd go *ow-wow-wow!* like that, and I'd go, *Huh! serves you right, rotten robber. You shouldn't go around stealing things. Dazzy Donut Dog is on your case!* Then they'd run away, slowly, because they only have two naff legs.

So there I was, the superest, dooperest guard dog ever, and right now, right there in front of me, almost touching my nose and almost almost almost in my mouth even – there were all these pies and sausage rolls just lying there. I could almost hear them calling out to me: *Hey, we're over here, lots of lovely pies just ready to be stolen!*

STUPID PIES! So I thought, right, I will be Dazzy Donut Dog and get in the back of this van

and stand guard over it. I shall probably get a
medal for doing this and meet the Queen, but I
hope she doesn't pin it on me because that would
make me jump. It would have to be on a ribbon.
A yellow one.

And I'd probably get a reward too, like a
lifetime's supply of pies and I could take it back
for my three puppies, because they are the best
puppies IN THE WHOLE WORLD and I love
them to bits and pieces of bits. Then my pups
would know what a brave and clever mum they
have and guess who that is? ME!

That was why I got in the back of the van. There I was, busily checking it out to make sure there wasn't a pie thief hiding somewhere, and what did I find? A big sausage roll, on the floor. In fact, not just one, but three sausage rolls, lying ON THE FLOOR! How stupid can a sausage roll get? That's asking for trouble, isn't it?

I said, 'Hello, hello. What are you lot doing out of your box?' And I was about to pick one up and put it with the others when I thought: *Hmmm, this might be a pretend sausage roll.*

I know you can get pretend pies because I ate one once. It was a mistake. I didn't mean to eat it. At least, that's not exactly true – I DID mean to eat it but that was because I thought it was a real pie, but it turned out to be made of painted plastic. It tasted horrible and I had to spit it out. SPLUUURRRRGH! Like that.

All these splinters of plastic came shooting out of my mouth and made a mess and lots of people shouted at me and I got chased (again), but I

didn't care because I can run like a crazy thing,
like a rocket, like an un-guided missile. In fact, I
am probably the fastest dog in the whole world.
(Though I'm not very good at stopping.) Besides,
they shouldn't make plastic pies. What is the
point of that?!

Anyway, I thought: *This roll could be like that nasty
pie and there's only one way I know to check if the sausage
roll is real and that is to taste it.*

2 The Pie Robber

I picked up one of the rolls with my teeth. It certainly felt like a sausage roll. That was the first good sign. And it certainly smelt like a sausage roll. That was the second good sign, so I licked it all over just to make sure, and it certainly tasted like a sausage roll, and that was the best sign of all.

I looked at the roll and the roll looked at me and I was thinking: *Aha! Suppose it only tastes like a sausage roll on the outside, but the inside is made of something horrible, like mustard, or custard?* Well, there's only one way to check for that, so I bit into it, and guess what? It wasn't made of custard or mustard. It was made of sausage. Right the way through.

The roll was a bit chewed up by this time
so I thought I might as well swallow it. Then I
checked the other two sausage rolls that were
lying on the floor to make sure they weren't
pretending, and guess what? They weren't. So
that meant the only thing to do was to stay there
and guard the rest of the pies and rolls and make
sure that nobody came along and tried to eat
them.

That was when I had my CLEVER IDEA.
Now then, Trevor Two-Legs gets pocket money
and he puts it in a piggy bank to keep it safe from

robbers. So my clever idea was this. I thought:
*I can put all those pies in a special bank for pies, and then
nobody can steal them.* I haven't got a piggy bank,
but I do have a doggy bank. In fact, I AM a
doggy bank!

Wasn't that a brilliant idea?! So I started eating
as many pies and rolls as I could so they would
be safe. Then I saw a two-legs coming towards
the back of the van. He was a SAUSAGE ROLL
ROBBER! I know he was a robber because he
was wearing dark glasses. This was going to be
my big moment. I'd definitely get a medal and a
lifetime's supply of pies for this!

I crouched down behind a crate and got ready
to growl and bark and leap up and throw myself
at his ankles and go RAARGH! RAARGH!

The thing was though, the man didn't steal any
pies or sausage rolls. All he did was shut the door.
BANG! And I was still inside. I felt him climb
into the front of the van and the engine started
up and we were off. VROOOM!

He wasn't supposed to do that! He wasn't supposed to steal the whole van! He was only supposed to steal the pies! I shall never understand two-legs. What was the point in taking the whole van when all he had to do was reach inside and take the pies from the back?

We rattled off down the road and I was wondering what to do. I soon realized that my first duty as a guard dog was to protect the rest of the rolls and pies and get them safe inside my doggy bank. So I ate them, which meant getting them out of their boxes and everything. I'm so clever!

Then I barked and barked, *woof-woof-WOOF*!
But the driver man didn't hear me. I threw
myself at the back wall of the cab. I leaped at it
and scritch-scratched it and bit it and barked, but
it was no use. HE WAS DEAF!

Two-legs have got terrible hearing. Not like me.
I can hear ants snoring when it's ant bedtime. But
two-legs always have such silly, small ears – have
you noticed? It's no wonder they can't hear
properly. Mine are big and flappy like proper ears
should be. And my pups have got ears like flags!

I tried to sit down, but the van was on wriggly
roads. I got thrown all over the place and soon
I felt a bit sick. I'm sure it wasn't the pies, it was
the van, and before long I really was sick. I was
a bit miffed at first because I thought my plan
wouldn't work now, because half the rolls and
pies were back on the van floor, even if they
were a bit mushy. But then I remembered how
picky two-legs are when it comes to food. They
probably wouldn't want them now. Not when

they were all gloopy and steaming.

We travelled for ages. It felt like about a year at least and it had gone dark too. The van slowed down and squeaked to a stop. I went and hid behind a crate so I could leap out at the robber and go RAARGH! RAARGH!

The back door opened. I peeped out. The two-legs was bald and he'd taken off his dark glasses. I thought: *That's odd. He doesn't look so robber-ish now.* As he opened the door he staggered back, holding his nose and staring at the brown piles on the van floor. I thought: *Aha, this is my moment of glory! I shall get a medal and meet the Queen!*

So in my head I ate a super-special-power donut and became the wonderfully brave and fearless Dazzy Donut Dog. I hurled myself out from behind the crate and I started to go RAARGH! RAARGH! but my tummy was still feeling upset from the ride and I threw up instead, all down his trousers. He screamed like a lady with a big spider and, well, I know that kind

of scream. It means trouble, so I ran for it as fast as I could, which was a lot faster than him with only two naff legs and I disappeared into the night. Ha ha! I am so clever sometimes.

And then I discovered where I was. Or to put it another way, I discovered where I wasn't. It was the middle of nowhere. I was hopelessly LOST.

3 The Middle of Nowhere

What a dark and moonless night! It was a bit creepy, I can tell you. The wind howled and an owl hooted. They are such old ladies, owls. All they ever do is go *Whoo-hoooo!* like they're scared of the dark. Why don't they get up during the day when the sun's shining? I'm not scared of the dark at all because Dazzy Donut Dog is not scared of ANYTHING.

It was eerily quiet, apart from that daft owl. I wandered along a wide, empty street with big buildings. They were even bigger than the building I ran into last week by mistake. I'd never seen so many books. I got chased out by three screaming women and one of them tried to hit me with a magazine and I hadn't even done

anything! Anyhow she missed, because I am the superest dog at zigzagging and can run like a TORNADO!

The buildings were lit by orange lights and surrounded by tall wire fences. The fences had big signs with pictures on. Sometimes it was a skull, and sometimes it was a two-legs being struck by lightning and it was making him jump-jump-jump, like he was going *Ooh! Ow! Stop it!*

I knew what those signs meant – they meant
DANGER! KEEP OUT!

I sat down so I could have a thinking kind of
scratch. I scratched behind my right ear and
under my chin. I scratched my chest and the
top of my head and behind my left ear. Then I
scratched in front of my left ear, and the funny
thing was, I still didn't know where I was.
I thought: *There must be a sensible way to do this.*

What I need to do is start with what I already know. It will be like putting the pieces of a puzzle together.

So I started sorting things out, like this:

Question 1:   Where am I?

Answer: I don't know.

Question 2:   Which direction is home?

Answer: I don't know.

Question 3:   Are there any pies left?

Answer: I don't know. The van's gone now and anyway, what have pies got to do with finding your way home?

Question 4:   You've ruined it now. You've just asked a question and it was supposed to be an answer.

Answer: And now you've given an answer when you were supposed to be asking a question.

Question 5:   Will you stop doing things the wrong way round?

Answer: Oh good, that was a proper

	question. Ask me another.
Question 6:	If you don't know the way home, how can you find out?
Answer:	Ask someone.
Question 7:	That's a really good idea.
Answer:	That isn't a question. That's just conversation.

After that I got tired of talking to myself and decided I really couldn't do anything more until it was morning so I started to look for somewhere to sleep.

I hunted and hunted but everywhere was just roads and big buildings with hardly any windows, and wire fencing. I walked right round to see if there might be a place where I could get in. I came to some enormous gates covered with skulls and people getting hit by lightning and going *Ooh! Ow! Stop it!* I sat down and wondered why nobody was allowed in.

Anyhow, I was sitting there, wondering where

I could sleep, when all at once two gigantic massive monster mutts as big as rhinoceroses came thundering across and hurled themselves at me from the other side of the chain-link fence.

Well! I just sat there and looked at them. I mean, what was all THAT about? Couldn't they see the wire? They clawed at it with their paws and foam was bubbling out of their mouths. They rolled their bloodshot eyes and growled like nothing on earth. 'GRR$%&*@RRR!' Honestly, the language they used! It was dreadful.

'Good evening,' I replied, bccause I think if you're polite then there's no reason for anyone to get upset.

And they said: 'Why don't you *&^%$£ back to your wormhole you @£$%^& *&^%$ %£$^%&*@**% *&^%$£@'

'Oh, really?' I answered coolly. 'Well, the trouble, dear friends, is that I'm afraid you don't have any brains.'

You should have seen them! They went crazy-mad! They launched themselves at the fence again, roaring and cursing – it was such bad language. I got to my feet and walked up and down in front of them.

'I say, you chaps, haven't you noticed that there's a four-metre-high chain-link fence between us, which YOU CAN'T GET THROUGH? What's all the fuss about, you BONE-HEADED CLOD-PODS? Look at you, all big and muscly and foaming at the mouth, and you can't do anything because YOU'RE ON

THE OTHER SIDE OF THE FENCE, TWIT-POODLES!'

Then I began to copy their barking and went: 'OH, WOOF WOOFY WOOF. I'M A BIG BAD DOG WITH NO BRAINS. WOOF WOOF.'

They got so mad they tried to climb up the fence! They did! Completely crazy, the pair of them. And then this big, fat, two-legs guard came out of his hut to see what all the fuss was about. He tried to shoo me away by shouting and saying stupid things to me like 'Go home, you daft dog!' And I shouted back at him that I most certainly would go home if only I knew where it was, but of course he couldn't understand me because he was a two-legs, with small ears.

Mr Security was shining his torch in my face and banging the fence with his night-stick and yelling, and his two stupid monster mutts kept on barking. They were all so annoying and guess what I did? I was really cool! I went up to the

fence, right in front of them, and piddled through the wire on to Mr Security's boots. Ha ha ha!

That was when he opened the gates and let his dogs out. Oops!

4 Whoo-hoo!

Fortunately I am the fastest dog on the planet
and I switched on my turbo super-dooper-
pooper-charger and went ZOOOOM! It was the
last I saw of them and soon I'd left the buildings
far behind.

That was a bit of an adventure, but I still didn't
have anywhere to sleep and now I was *really* in
the middle of nowhere. I wandered around for
a while and eventually I found an old cardboard
box lying beside a hedge so I crawled beneath it.

It was ages before I got to sleep. I kept thinking
about home and my gorgeous pups with their
floppy sloppy tongues, and Trevor. He hasn't got
a floppy sloppy tongue of course but he's good
fun and I can play with him and take him for

walks. We make a good team, Trevor and me.
I even help with his homework sometimes. He
had a problem with triangles the other night
and he had to ask me because it was a difficult
problem.

'Listen, Streaker, the question says: *What do you
call a triangle with two equal sides?*'

Well! That's a stupid question, isn't it? I mean,
you can't call a triangle anything except a triangle,
can you? You can't call it biscuit or walkies or
donuts can you? It's a triangle – so that's what you
call it.

Trevor read the question over and he got more
and more angry and eventually he shouted at his
homework.

'You call it a triangle! Because that's what it is,
stupid!'

See? That's what I'd said too! I love helping
Trevor, and we think triangles are stupid. And
they are too.

Anyway, if I'd been at home I would probably

be lying on the end of Trevor's bed with my pups and he'd be snoring, because he does, even if he is only eleven. Sometimes he sounds like a road drill.

I don't mind him snoring because that means he's deeply asleep. Then I can creep up the bed and lie right next to him because I don't see why he should have all the cushy pillows while I only get the bottom bit next to his smelly feet. Besides, if his snoring gets too loud, I climb on top of his head and he stops. That's because he can't breathe. Then all of a sudden he gives a big jerk, mutters *Gerroff*, turns over and goes back to sleep.

Gerroff!

But I wasn't at home and I didn't have Trevor to cuddle up to, and I didn't have my puppies. I was under an old, damp cardboard box that stank of cranky-manky soap, a long way from home – wherever that was. All on my own.

When I did get to sleep at last I was immediately woken up by that stupid owl. It landed on top of the box and scrabbled about going scritch-scratch until my brain went banana-bonkers.

'For heaven's sake,' I muttered. 'Stop tap dancing.'

Then it started making silly owl noises. 'Whooo. Whoo-hoooooo.'

'Whoo-hoo to you too,' I wuffed back.

Silence. A minute passed.

'Did you speak?' whispered the owl.

'Yes, I told you to stop tap dancing.'

'Whooooooooo!' went the owl. 'A talking box!'

'Oh, please,' I groaned. 'I'm a dog!'

'Whooooooo! A talking box that thinks it's a dog!'

'Will you please stop whoo-hoo-ing and go
away and find a bit of brain to put in your head?'

'WHOOOOOOOOOOOO!' went the owl, so I
decided to get up.

Of course I was still under the box so I ended
up wandering round wearing a box over my head
and back, with a large owl riding on top and
whoooo-ing with alarm. I barked at it until it flew
off. Hooray. That's owls for you. They are the
stupidest birds ever. Blackbirds sing. Thrushes

sing. Robins sing. What do owls do? They go 'whoooooo', and sound like someone stuck in a wardrobe with a family of giant bats.

I settled back down, fell asleep and had the weirdest dream. I was running, running, running and panting madly. My eyes were bulging. Something was chasing me. A big, black shadow. Why was it so scary? It was a shadow galloping behind me, like I was being chased by a piece of night. There was a strange, hot smell in my nostrils, like somewhere far away and dangerous.

I was running as fast as I could but it felt like my feet were stuck in donut jam, and my puppies were calling out to me, 'Mum! Mum! Save us!' My heart was thundering and I woke by leaping to my feet, my eyes wide. I couldn't see! I'd gone blind! Terror seized me.

Then I realized I still had the cardboard box tipped over my head. I shook myself free and stared out at the coming dawn, panting, heart racing. There was nothing to be seen except a

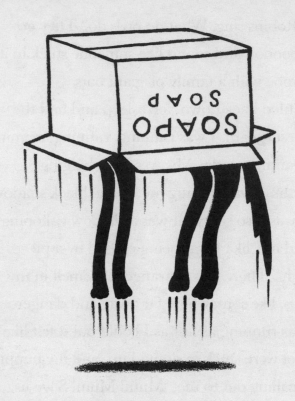

cold streak of light low down in the east. A new
day.

I was glad to be awake. I don't want to have
another dream like that. Not ever.

5 In the Company of a Killer

I woke up so hungry I could have eaten a
hippopotamus, but there wasn't one. Just as
well really. They're a lot bigger than I am.
I was desperate for food. A dog like me needs
regular meals. If I'd been at home Trevor Two-
Legs would have put a big bowl of something
scrummy-yummy in front of me. And if I'd been
in a town it would have been easy. There's always
lots of nosh lying about because those two-legs,
they drop stuff, and also there are litter bins. And
also also also there is daylight robbery. (Which I
am quite good at.)

You hang around a food shop and when
nobody is looking you snaffle a roast chicken or
something. Do you know what the best target is?

I will tell you – a two-legs coming out of a burger bar. There they are stepping through the doorway with a big, fat burger and they're trying to cram it into their big, fat mouth. Easy nosh!

You have to plan this and time everything just right. This is how it's done:

1. Check distance to door. Allow at least five metres.

2. Chcck area for any two-legs. Make
   sure you have a clear run to the door
   and a clear getaway. Don't let any
   two-legs get in the way.
3. Check timing.

Timing is really important. The two-legs with
the burger has to be lifting the bun to his mouth
at the right speed and the right time. If they are
then that's your moment. Your paws scrabble
madly on the pavement, *whizz-whizz-whizz*, and
you hurl yourself forward like an Outer-Space-
Galaxy-Fighter-Rocket-Plane on a bombing
run to blow up the Death-Star-Thingy-Whatsit
– *FWWOWWWWW*!

Three bounds and you have reached top
speed and now you launch yourself through the
air, flying in a graceful arc and you dive right
between two-legs's face and the paw with the
burger. With a tiny neat twist of your head you
snatch the Death-Star-Thingy-burger from his

paw just before it disappears into his mouth and you're away! You land on the far side and you're off at top speed, whoosh-whizz, chomping the burger as you go. Job done. Yum yum yum!

I love doing that!

Just don't make the same mistake I did once. I waited in ambush outside a burger place. The door opened and out came a two-legs right in the act of raising the bun to his face. I ran, I jumped, I flew, I grabbed, I landed and made off chewing happily. Chomp chomp chomp! But guess what? It wasn't a burger bun at all. It was a mobile phone, and instead of a scrummy burger I had a strange voice in my mouth going 'Urrh? Is that you, Harry? Harry? Are you growling? What's that chomping noi–'

Then the phone went dead. That was because I'd just killed it and spat it out. Splrrrrgh! Mobiles are not good to eat, I promise you. They're even worse than plastic pies.

But you can't find burger bars in the middle of

nowhere. I was going to have to hunt. Maybe I'd
find a rabbit that didn't mind being my breakfast.
I mooched around here and I mooched around
there and do you know what? I think I must have
picked the only rabbit-less zone in the entire
country. There wasn't a single one. I was so fed
up and miserable and my tummy was saying: *Feed
me! Please feed me! There's space for an elephant in here!*
And that was when the cat fell on me.

I was passing beneath a tree when there was

a startled yowl from above and as I looked up a large ginger ball of fur came zonking out of the tree, bounced off my head, landed on the ground, got up and looked at me with raised eyebrows.

'Hi . . .' it began. Then it saw my teeth and my hungry smile and decided to run for its life. I decided to run for its life too. I mean, you have to if you're a dog. Cats and dogs are ancient enemies. We chase and they run. So that's what we did.

Whoosh! I've never seen a cat run so fast! And zig and zag! Away across the field we went, with my ears streaming out behind me – I love that! – until all of a sudden the cat stopped dead, spun round, hissed, spat and lashed out with one paw and almost took my head off as I skidded to a halt.

'Whoa!' I yelled, leaping back. 'What was that for?'

'I'm fed up with running,' snarled the cat, with

every single hair on its body standing up and its tail all fluffed up until it looked like a monkey puzzle tree. Bristling – that's what it was doing.

I sat down and stared at it. The cat glared back, lifted one paw, casually flicked open its claws and began to clean between them with its teeth. 'So,' drawled the cat. 'What are you going to do now, clever-clogs?'

Good point. What was I going to do? I opened my mouth to speak, didn't know what to say, so I shut it again. The cat grinned.

'Lost for words? That's the trouble with you dogs. You're all hurry-scurry, huff, puff and woof.' The cat's fur slowly smoothed itself and he sat back on his haunches, never taking his golden eyes off me. Unnerving, it was, I can tell you. I decided to play it casual and act as if I knew what I was doing.

'Actually, I was looking for a burger bar,' I announced. The cat fell over laughing. He wasn't meant to do that. Where was the respect? Down the drain, that's where it was.

The cat glanced round. 'A burger bar, in a field? Of course you were. Tell me, was I born an idiot, or were you born an idiot? Don't bother to answer.'

'Are you always as rude as this?' I asked tetchily.

'Only if you're as stupid as this.'

I ask you! That's no way to speak to Dazzy Donut Dog. 'Listen, chum, I could crunch up your head in one gulp.'

'You could,' agreed the cat, lying down and

rolling on to its back as if it didn't much care what I did but I could rub its tummy if I liked. 'But before that happened I would probably have taken out both your eyes, shredded your nose and stuffed carrots into your ears.'

I choked. 'Why would you stuff carrots into my ears?'

'I always do,' said the cat casually. 'It's my signature. Murderers always leave a signature on the dead body. Don't you know anything? The Deadly Daffodil used to leave a daffodil next to his victim. Wanda the Weasel always left a lipstick kiss-print on her prey's cheek. I stuff carrots in their ears.'

I swallowed hard. I was in the company of a killer cat. I began to back away. The cat smiled again.

'You believe me, don't you?' it purred. 'I said you were stupid. Where on earth do you think I'm going to find carrots around here?'

'I knew you were joking,' I shouted.

'Of course you did. So then, tell me, Mr Mutt, what *are* you doing round here?'

'I'm lost. And I'm not Mr Mutt. I'm a Miss and my name's Streaker.'

The cat stretched itself slowly. 'Well, Streaker, you may call me Great Lord and Master of All Things Visible and Invisible; Emperor of the Woods, the Wilds, the Winds and Wobbly Things; Pendragon of all Hilly Bits; Sultan of Sausages; Celestial Prince of Kippers, Goldfish and Chunky Rabbit –'

'How about Moggy?' I interrupted.

'I don't think so, unless you want to see those carrots,' snapped the cat.

'I'll call you Cat.'

He eyed me for a second. 'It's a deal,' he agreed. 'I hate those names two-legs give you. I used to be called Sweety-pie.'

'Bit out of character,' I observed.

'Exactly. Have you had breakfast? No? I've got half a mouse somewhere. I'm a bit of a wanderer myself. My two-legs threw me out.'

I thought: *I'm not surprised. I've never met such a . . . such a catty cat.* I didn't say it of course. Didn't want my ears filled with carrots. I tried to sound sympathetic.

'Life must be hard,' I offered.

'I survive,' Cat said with a shrug as we wandered towards the hedge. 'But a warm home would be nice. Ah, there it is.'

He showed me the half mouse. It was the bottom half. I looked at the tail and the two back legs and I didn't feel nearly so hungry as I thought.

'It's kind of you to offer, but I'm not that fond of mice.'

Cat shrugged and gulped it down in one. 'We could head for town,' he suggested, as he cleaned his whiskers.

'Now that is a good idea. I can snaffle some food and maybe we can find out where we are and then work out how to get back home.'

'Excellent,' agreed Cat, trotting ahead of me, his tail held high. I fell in behind. I was thinking: *This is weird. I'm following a cat. It's like we're friends. I hope nobody sees. I'd be so ashamed. This isn't supposed to happen.* And then I thought: *I'm hungry.*

6 Flying Lessons

We heard the noise first – a steadily increasing
hum. I thought: *It's a giant bee as big as an elephant.
It will suddenly appear from nowhere and land on top of
us and we'll be squashed. Splat!*

I've had a bit of a problem with bees ever
since one stung my tongue. All I did was eat a
cheese sandwich. How was I to know there was
a bee inside trying to eat the cheesy bit? The
bee didn't like being eaten so it stung me. OW!
OUCH! HOT! My tongue was on fire! I went
racing round and round with my tongue hanging
out as far as possible, like I was trying to make
it fall right out of my mouth. I had to dash dash
dash all the way upstairs and stick my head in
the toilet bowl so I could plunge my tongue into

the water to cool it down. FLOBBA-DOBBA-
JOBBA! That was better.

I don't like bees, and the humming noise was
making me nervous. What would Dazzy Donut
Dog do? Aha! I soon had a cunning plan. I
trotted four steps and then suddenly leaped up,
spun round to face back and landed. Then I
walked backwards four steps, leaped up and spun
round, so I was facing forward once more. And
each time I spun round and landed I growled and

went *Raargh! Raargh! Gotcha!* just in case.

Cat stopped and watched me for several moments. 'Everything all right?' he asked casually.

'There's an elephant-bee,' I explained. 'So watch out.'

'There is no such thing as an elephant-bee except in your head,' said Cat. 'And if you carry on walking and spinning and not looking where you're going you will –'

CRUNCH! OW!

'Crash into the tree you've just crashed into,' Cat continued evenly.

I sat under the tree, nursing my bruised nose and chin. Life can be really horrible sometimes. There I was, trying to avoid an elephant-bee, and I get attacked by a tree instead. I glared at the trunk. *Raargh!* There. That showed it.

'Come and look at this,' called Cat. 'I think we've reached somewhere.'

We had come to the edge of a huge pit. The ground just fell away from our feet. Cat and I stood right on the edge, staring down at the bustling scene below. A steady hum rose from the pit – the elephant-bee!

Crowds of pea-sized two-legs hurried about. They popped in and out of cars which swooshed and swished, pooping and parping at each other like hundreds of cross babies crawling round a giant playpen. In the middle of all this was a glittering glass city with a hundred doors that opened and shut, opened and shut, letting out crowds and sucking in eager throngs.

'What is it?' I whispered to Cat.

'Have you never seen a shopping centre before?'

I shook my head, and at the same time a vague memory came back to me. Trevor and his parents used to talk about going to the shopping centre, though they never took me. Maybe it was the same one.

MAYBE IT WAS THE SAME ONE!

And if it WAS the same one then maybe I wasn't far from HOME and MAYBE if we went down to the shopping centre we wouldn't just find FOOD we might see TREVOR! What's more, if we saw Trevor he would take me home and I'D BE WITH MY PUPPIES AGAIN! And I'd pull their ears and bite their tails and they are so yummy I could almost eat them because I love them so much.

'Let's go!' I woofed and set off down the side of the hill as fast as possible. Funnily enough, 'as fast as possible' turned out to be very fast indeed, because it wasn't actually the side of a hill at all, it was a cliff face!

'Stop, you idiot!'

I heard Cat yell after me, but by that time I was already tumble-rumble-rolling down and down. And the tumble-rumble became a bouncy-bounce and all of a sudden I WAS FLYING!

Fantastic! And then, and then, and THEN
I realized I wasn't actually flying – I was
FALLING!

AND I DIDN'T HAVE A PARACHUTE!
I WAS CRASHING!
And then guess what?
I CRASHED! I HIT THE GROUND!
KERRUMPPP!
(Oof! Ow! Bish! Bash! Oooh! Urgh! Wallop!
Wapp! Eek! Squeak!)

That must have been my fastest crish-
crash-crush ever. Wow! I got to my feet rather
unsteadily and counted my legs to make sure
none of them had fallen off and do you know
something? I had five! But the fifth one was
just my tail being sad and hanging down. So I
wagged it and woofed: 'Ta da!' because I was
so amazed at myself. A small crowd of two-legs
gathered round.

'Giraffe!' cried a child, pointing at me. I shook my head sadly. Honestly, kids these days – they don't know anything. I blame the schools.

'You need glasses, I'm a dog,' I snapped back, even though I knew they wouldn't understand. Why is it that two-legs spend so much time teaching us to understand *them*, but they never bother to learn *our* language?

'Psst!'

I swung round. It was Cat. He was lurking

behind a litter bin. He jerked his head to say I should follow him, so I did.

'Excuse me, ladies and gentlemen,' I wuffled, trotting after him and a moment later we legged it for some cover in one of the car parks.

'Do you make a habit of throwing yourself off cliffs?' Cat asked.

'I was flying,' I told him.

'You were not flying. If you want to fly you have to wear an aeroplane. You could have been killed.'

'Well I wasn't, so there. How did you get down then?'

'I used the path that was right next to where you decided to make your Death Leap,' Cat said icily.

'I flew.'

Cat sighed and suggested we went on a food hunt. I said we could look for Trevor Two-Legs at the same time. I was certain that this must be the shopping centre that he came to with his parents, and I also knew in my heart of heart of hearts that Trevor would be LOOKING FOR ME!

7 Found?

We decided to begin our search round the back.
Cat thought it would be safer if we kept away
from the two-legs and he was probably right.
Behind the shops it was pretty filthy. Shops looks
clean and shiny from the front, but you should
see the back. It's all cardboard boxes and piles of
rubbish thrown out every which way.

I could smell food so I followed my nose, sniff-
sniffing until I reached a dark doorway. The door
was open. I went in. Cat hovered behind me.

'Is it safe?' he asked.

'Scaredy-cat,' I threw back at him.

'Not,' he said, stepping inside. 'I was checking
my whiskers. Cats' whiskers are very sensitive,
you know.'

We headed up a short corridor and soon found ourselves peering into a huge glass palace. I hardly knew where to look there was so much to see. Everywhere you turned there was something different – clothes shops, food shops, kitchen shops, books, TVs, magazines, computers – all spread out on two levels connected by moving stairways and there were two-legs everywhere! It reminded me of an ants' nest I dug up once by mistake, when I was trying to bury a bone.

'I don't like it,' muttered Cat. 'I don't trust them.'

'Listen, where there are two-legs there's always free food. It's Rule Number Two.'

'What's Rule Number One?'

'Rule Number One is there's no such thing as a free lunch.'

'Doesn't that contradict Rule Number Two?' asked Cat.

'Does it?'

Cat shook his head. 'Dogs,' he muttered.

'Brains like mushy peas.'

I wasn't going to let him get away with an insult like that! 'Cats,' I shot back. 'Brains like triangles.'

Cat stopped dead. 'What?'

Honestly! Don't you hate it when you make a really clever remark but nobody understands? It happens to me a lot. I flicked my tail casually. 'Oh, come on! Everyone knows triangles are stupid.'

Cat went on staring at me. 'Really? Oh.'

He shook his head and I pressed ahead.

'Come on, I can smell food.'

We soon found a really brilliant butcher's, piled high with whopping great lumps of the meatiest meat ever, just dying to be gobbled up at once. My tongue was almost trailing on the floor. And guess what? They had a whole tray of salami sausages. My favourite. I love garlic!

I was about to tell Cat that he ought to do something to attract everyone's attention while I sneaked up on the salami, when double guess what?

I SAW TREVOR! AND MR TWO-LEGS!

They were on the other side of the store, on the upper level! I jumped for joy. I jumped so much I landed on top of the meat counter and woofed as loudly as I could: 'I'M OVER HERE!'

Trevor turned and looked. Mr Two-Legs turned and looked. They saw me. They jumped for joy too and yelled back: 'STREAKER! WE'RE OVER HERE!'

'I KNOW YOU'RE OVER THERE! I SAW YOU FIRST!'

Then I realized that it wasn't just Trevor and Mr Two-Legs looking at me — it was everyone and they were all staring at me standing on the meat counter. They didn't look happy at

all. Somebody began to reach out with big red grabby paws and I thought: *I know what you want to do. You're going to take me away from Trevor and my puppies and I shan't let you.* So I went *woof-woof-raaargh!* and that scared them so much they looked like bananas in a liquidizer. Then all the two-legs began screaming and leaping up and down. It was time to scarper and we set off down the hall.

Talk about yelling! Anyone would think I was

a giant cockroach! Several people jumped on to counters and clung to each other in horror. One woman grabbed a ceiling light and she went swinging backwards and forwards until she ran out of grip and let go and she landed on the egg display – KER-SPLOPPETY-SPLAP!

'Ohhh, a doggy!'

'Oooh, a kitty!'

'Get them out at once!'

'Call the Fire Brigade!'

'Get Pest Control!'

Pest Control? That was a bit much. Cat was looking more and more worried as the two-legs began to close in around us. I desperately hunted round for Trevor. Then I saw him. He was still with his dad and they were struggling down the moving stairs, pushing against the crowds of shoppers trying to escape from all the fuss and bother below.

'TREVOR!' I woofed.

'STREAKER! I'M COMING!'

Cat was pulling at me. 'We've got to go. Come on, it's too dangerous. The two-legs are almost on top of us. WE HAVE TO GO NOW BEFORE IT'S TOO LATE!'

'TREVOR!' I bellowed.

But this time there was no answer and no sign of either of them. Strange hands were beginning to pull at me. It was definitely time to be Dazzy Donut Dog again, and I secretly ate two imaginary super-dooper-power-plus Dazzy Donuts with all those little coloured sprinkles on top.

KER-CHINNGGG!

I struggled free, forced myself to turn away and raced after Cat, who was already legging it. Faster and faster we went, until my ears were streaming out behind me. We skidded between counters. We knocked displays over. We knocked people over. Everywhere we went the shouts and yells followed close behind. Now it had become a race for freedom.

We dashed up the 'down' escalator, and down the 'up' escalator. We raced through a bedding store, using the display of beds like trampolines – *boyoinngg! boyoinngg! boyoinngg!* We toppled wardrobes so the two-legs had to clamber over them to get to us.

We hurled ourselves through a big clothing store and Cat came out at the other end wearing a pair of pink knickers over his head. We raced past the electrical area and I got a vacuum cleaner plug caught up in my collar and now I was towing a big red vacuum cleaner along behind me. The vacuum cleaner got caught on a display of handbags and soon I had this huge trail of bits and bobs bouncing and skidding along behind me until at last the plug worked free and I shot off after Mr Frilly Knickers.

I could see the open doors that meant escape. 'This way!' I yelled at Cat. We even had to dash back past the butcher's on the way and I got that salami sausage! A leap, a snaffle and it was mine! *Whoosh-whizz!* I am so good at this! There is no dog like me anywhere in the universe! I am the world champion. Even better than Dazzy Donut Dog, probably.

We went whooshing back outside and a furious pile of two-legs came tumbling after us like lava spilling from a volcano.

'Get the thieves!'

We whizzed out into the open air and across the road, still scattering shoppers. There was a wild chorus of poops and parps from cars, several screeching skids and a series of loud bangs as they crashed into one another. Doors were flung open and drivers leaped out but they were instantly mown down by the unstoppable crowd that was chasing us from the centre. What a kerfuffle! Someone started a fight and it quickly spread.

Cat and I crept quietly away and hid beneath

a big wheelie bin. In the distance we heard sirens approaching. We split the salami sausage between us. Cat chomped happily on his while I just sat there, looking out at the disaster area beyond. It was my last chance to spot Trevor. I couldn't believe that we had found each other and then lost each other again. And it wasn't just Trevor I'd lost. It was my pups. They seemed further away than ever.

Cat's head jerked up from his sausage. 'Are you sniffling?' he asked.

'No,' I growled. 'Dazzy Donut Dog does not sniffle.'

Cat lowered his head and began chewing again. 'Lovely salami,' he said cheerfully. 'Mind if I eat yours?'

8 How to Read

We stayed under the wheelie bin for the rest of the day. For one thing we were sleeping, and for another it took a long time to clear away the mess. Breakdown trucks towed away the smashed vehicles, one by one. Those two-legs can make VERY BIG MESSES when they want to. If I made a mess that big I would be in such trouble.

It was late afternoon when we moved. It had started to drizzle. The problem was that there were roads leaving the shopping centre in every direction. Which one should we follow? I sniffed around for clues but there was nothing helpful, only messages from other dogs, some cats, a fox and a new, weird scent that neither of us could make sense of.

'Foreign language,' Cat said eventually. 'Polish probably.'

Cat and I spotted a road sign, with its funny picture and writing. Cat frowned and nodded wisely.

BARTON
&
FARKLE

TRAPHAM
SAFARI PARK

'Do you know what it says?' I asked Cat in astonishment. 'Can you read?'

'Of course,' Cat said nodding. 'All cats can read.'

'Really?'

'Of course. Cats can do anything.'

This was good news. I'd always thought cats were idiots. I looked at him with admiration. 'What does it say?'

'Seven o'clock,' Cat announced.

'Oh.' I was disappointed. I had hoped it would tell us where we were and where we should go. 'It doesn't say where Barton is? That's where Trevor lives.'

Cat shook his head. 'Nope. Just says seven o'clock. Come on, I reckon we should go right.'

I was puzzled. 'Why would a road sign say seven o'clock?' I asked Cat. He looked at me and rolled his eyes.

'How should I know? It's a sign for two-legs. You know how weird they are. Maybe they need to know when it's seven o'clock. Look, it's raining. We're getting wet. Are you coming or not?'

I trotted after him. Sometimes Cat made me feel small and stupid. I didn't like that. I'm not small and stupid. I'm middle-sized and parts of me are clever. I'd like to see Cat snatch a salami from the middle of a shopping centre.

However, it was good to have a friend to travel with and it was brilliant that he could read. That was going to prove a big help. We edged along the roundabout and took the road on the right.

We kept going until it was dark, by which time the rain was really coming down and we were both soaked. Cat likes the night more than I do. It's good for pouncing, he says. The darker it is, the better. Personally speaking, I prefer the moon, and the brighter it is, the better. So we argued and almost had a fight. I went *raargh-raargh* and showed Cat my teeth and he went *hiss-hiss* and flicked open the claws on one paw. We stood and glared at each other for a few moments and then decided to call it a draw. It was a stupid argument anyway. We only did it because we were fed up, cold and wet.

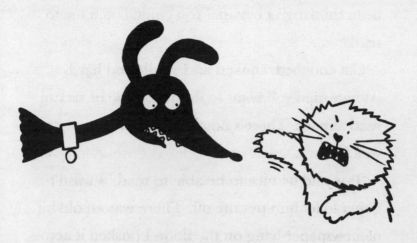

Not long after that we found a big old shed and decided to hole up there for the night. It was lovely to find somewhere dry. Cat caught two mice in the pitch dark. I couldn't even *see* them, but he could. He offered one to me but I wasn't interested so he ate one and said he'd have the other for pudding later. First of all he chucked them about the place a lot and chased after them.

'Why do you do that?' I asked. 'Why don't you just catch them and eat them?'

'Aerobics,' he said. 'Keeps me fit.'

I waited until the chewing had stopped. 'I've been thinking,' I began. 'You could teach me to read.'

Cat coughed, choked and swallowed hard. 'Why would you want to do that? One of us can read already. There's no point in you learning as well.'

'It would be nice to be able to read.' I wasn't going to let him put me off. There was an old bit of newspaper lying on the floor. I pushed it across to him and pointed to a word in big letters.

BOX

'What does that say?' I asked. 'How does it work? It looks so mysterious.'

Cat grumbled to himself and studied the word carefully. After a few moments he sat up neatly and poked the paper with one paw.

'It's quite simple,' he purred. 'Each of these

marks is a little picture and when you put each
little picture together it tells a story.'

'Really? That's wonderful!'

'Hmmm. The round one is an easy one. What
do you think it looks like?'

'The moon.'

'Don't be daft. It's too small to be the moon.
It's got to be something smaller.'

'Your head?'

'Do you want to learn how to read, or not?'

'Tell me what it is then.'

'It's an orange. So that mark means orange.'

'That's so clever! What do the other marks mean?'

Cat pointed at the last one. 'That's easy too.'

'It's a cross,' I said.

'Exactly. So that's what it means. Cross.'

'I'm beginning to get it!' I woofed excitedly. 'But I don't understand the first one. That looks difficult.'

'It's a bit hard,' agreed Cat. 'But if you're intelligent it's actually quite easy.'

I sat up and tried to be intelligent but it sounded like nonsense to me. How could it be hard and easy at the same time? I told Cat he'd have to explain.

'It's a picture of a two-legs,' Cat said. 'The two-legs is sitting down, so you can't see his legs. What you can see is his very fat belly and his even fatter bottom.'

'Yes. I can see that now, but it still doesn't make

sense. What is the story about?'

'It says *Two-legs is very cross because he has a fat orange belly and a fat orange bottom.*'

'It's a funny story!' I barked. 'Tell me another!'

'No. I'm tired. I'm going to sleep.' Cat closed his eyes and turned his back to me. I gazed at the wonderful story and my wonderful friend. Imagine being able to read stories like that! Cat was so clever. I closed my eyes.

9 An Unwelcome Visitor

Not for long. We were woken by the noise. I'd
heard that noise before. It was the noise very soft
feet make, like Trevor when he's creep-creeping
down to the kitchen to snaffle biscuits when he
thinks nobody's looking.

Cat's eyes were wide wide wide now. I'd never
seen them so big – great golden globes shining in
the black. His ears flicked this way and that and
went flat back against his head as he lowered his
body closer to the ground. His tail went switch-
twitch.

'Sssh!' he hissed.

'I didn't say anything,' I pointed out.

'You were breathing!'

'Well, I am SO sorry. Pardon me for living.'

'Sssh!' he hissed again urgently.

So we listened to the noiseless feet outside. Round the barn they padded and as the moon slid for a moment from behind a cloud WE SAW THE SHADOW – a BIG shadow moving across the open doorway and then it was gone, just leaving behind the strange scent of a faraway land. I was shivering. It wasn't cold. It was terror. I looked across at Cat, He was pressed hard against the ground, every hair on his body on end. We waited, and we waited some more. Whatever it was had gone. We took deeper breaths and at last I whispered, 'What was *that*?'

Cat's voice croaked with fear.

'The Beast. The Beast of the Night. It is a creature of the dark and uses night like a cloak of invisibility. It creeps upon its victim, seizes it and

that's the end of it. Terrifying.'

That sounded familiar to me. 'A bit like you catching mice?' I suggested. Cat's golden eyes slowly turned upon me and burned holes right through my skull.

'Or maybe like you chasing cats,' he suggested, slowly closing his eyes. 'The Beast is not a joke,' he went on. 'The Beast will eat anything, INCLUDING DOGS.'

I swallowed hard. 'Maybe I will have one of your mice after all,' I said. 'Then we can take

turns in keeping watch while the other sleeps.'
Cat smiled, flicked the second mouse across to
me and went to sleep.

I gazed at the dead mouse. Yuck! I wondered
what Dazzy Donut Dog would do. She'd never
have the problem in the first place. She'd be out
there, hunting The Beast. Then she would leap
upon it, RAARGH! RAARGH! BITE! CHOMP!
CHOMP! And The Beast would squeal like a
baby pig — oink-oink-oink — like that, in a teeny-tiny
voice. And The Beast would squeak: *Oh, please let
me go, Dazzy Donut Dog. You are so big and powerful
and scary and I won't ever be nasty again, not to anyone,
not even cats, not even worms, not even really eeny-weeny
things like woodlice.*

No. Dazzy Donut Dog would never-ever-ever-
in-a-million-years eat a dead mouse. So I didn't
either. Well, not for ten minutes anyway, but then
my stomach groaned with hunger. I shut my eyes
tight and said to myself: I am Dazzy Donut Dog
pouncing on The Beast and eating it all up. And I

went *raargh-raargh* and leaped on the mouse and sank my teeth into it and guess what? Cat jumped a billion miles into the sky because I'd missed the mouse and bitten his tail.

He was not impressed. In fact he swore at me. Yes, and very rude he was too. I didn't think cats knew words like that. He hissed and he spat and he didn't calm down until I'd said sorry about a trillion squillion times. Even then he went slinking off to a dark corner, jumped on to a rafter and slept up there, nursing his tail.

Which left me alone with the dead mouse. It was no good. I definitely could not eat a dead mouse. It was easy for Dazzy Donut Dog because she had special powers and could do ANYTHING, but I was just an ordinary doggy-type dog. I could not eat a dead mouse. Not even if I was as hungry as a hippopotamus.

My stomach lurched again. I wasn't as hungry as a hippo any more. Now I was as hungry as an elephant, maybe even as hungry as a blue whale. I bet an elephant or a blue whale wouldn't worry about eating a dead mouse. So I ate it – one bite and swallowed it whole. Gulp.

Then I closed my eyes and drifted off to sleep, with the rain drumming on the barn roof and dripping on to the floor. And I thought about my pups and Trevor and home. Oh yes, and pies. Mice taste horrible.

10 Dazzy Donut Dog Goes Surfing!

A wide river – and no bridge. That's what we had come to. Cat and I stared at the fast-flowing water. He asked me if I could swim. I carefully

explained, in woofs of one syllabark, that doggy paddle had been invented by dogs and that was why it was called doggy paddle. Cat took no notice of how witty I was being (which was VERY annoying of him) and carried on gazing at the rushing water.

'Can *you* swim?' I asked.

'All cats can swim,' muttered Cat. 'Cats can do anything.'

'OK then, let's go!' I shouted and we jumped in. I struck out for the opposite bank. From the corner of my eye I saw Cat swim rapidly downstream. He dived under. He reappeared. He dived under again. He came up. He went down. I thought maybe he had decided to go fishing, but he hadn't. He had decided to go drowning instead.

Cat surfaced for the fourth time spouting fountains of water into the air and waving his paws frantically at me. I paddled over to where he had just disappeared for the fifth time, dived

down, grabbed him by the tail and towed him to dry land. We were back where we'd started.

'You said you could swim,' I pointed out.

'I was. I was swimming downwards.'

'You were sinking.'

'I was diving.'

'Drowning.'

'I can swim,' Cat insisted. 'It's just that I haven't been taught yet.'

'That's nonsense. Admit it – you can't swim.'

'Can.'

'Can't.'

'I just need one or two lessons.'

'It's easy,' I told him. 'You just doggy paddle.'

'I'm a cat,' he pointed out a trifle heavily.

'In that case you catty paddle.' I thought it was funny, but Cat didn't like me rolling about on the grass in hysterics and he walked off in a huff, holding his bedraggled tail very stiffly so it might dry more quickly in the breeze. I followed him and offered to give him a piggyback.

'You can't,' he snapped back. 'You're not a pig. It would have to be a doggyback. Ha ha ha. Isn't that the funniest thing ever?'

'No,' I answered. 'And you're not laughing either.'

Cat sighed, sat down and eyed me in silence for a few moments. 'All right,' he said at last. 'I can't swim. You'll have to go on without me.'

I wasn't having that. Go on without Cat? No way! I needed him to read road signs and

things. I needed him to tell me
wonderful stories. I needed his
company. He was my friend.
Oh dear. A cat was my *friend*? I
hope nobody finds
out.

'We'll find a boat
or something,'
I suggested.

'Leave me. Go
and find your puppies. I'll be all right.' Pause.
'All on my own.' Pause. 'Alone.'

I hovered beside him. 'All we need is a boat.'

Cat lifted his head and gazed around. 'Oh yes.
Let's take one from the harbour.'

'Harbour?' I repeated.

'How about that nice ocean-going yacht? Or
would you prefer the luxury cruiser?'

I can be a bit slow sometimes, but the penny
dropped at last. Cat was being CATTY. I decided
to ignore it.

'I do like the cabin cruiser,' I said cheerfully, 'but it's a bit swanky. Maybe we can find a bit of plank or something.'

Good. That made Cat laugh and sit up. 'A bit of plank? I would feel a good deal safer on a whole plank, but if we have to make do with a bit then so be it.'

We padded up and down the river bank, hunting. At one point Cat stopped and stared at some tracks in the mud. He sniffed at them. I took a look.

'Big dog,' I said, but Cat shook his head.

'No claws.' Cat carefully placed his paw alongside the big print and pressed down into the mud. He left an almost exact copy of the big print, but a lot smaller.

'That's a cat's paw,' I said. 'But cats aren't that big.'

'The big ones are,' said Cat.

'There aren't any big ones,' I said.

'No,' Cat said slowly. 'There aren't *supposed* to

be any big ones.' He looked up at me. 'That,' he added, pointing at the track in the mud, 'is the mark of The Beast.'

I shivered. 'I think we'd better get across the river. As soon as possible. I'm beginning to think we're being followed.'

Ten minutes later we found a bit of plank. It wasn't all that long, but it was wide, and made a decent raft. We tried it out in the shallows first, just in case. Cat didn't like the river swishing over it from time to time, but the important thing was that it didn't sink, even when we both stood on it. We were ready to cross.

Cat stood at the front. I pushed forward and stepped on to the makeshift boat. We were instantly caught by the fast currents. We whirled and swirled, dipped, dashed and crashed through waves. Water surged across the plank and almost swept Cat away because he was lighter than me. His fur stood on end.

Our raft went hurtling down the river.

Sometimes we travelled forward, sometimes backwards, and sometimes we spun in wild circles, but at least we were on the move.

'Get it to the other side!' Cat yelled.

What did he think I could do? I had nothing to steer with. I dipped my tail into the water and tried to aim the boat at the opposite bank.

'That way!' Cat shouted. 'Rocks ahead! Watch out! Idiot!'

I was starting to panic. What would Dazzy

Donut Dog do? The answer came to me in a flash. Of course!

DAZZY DONUT DOG WAS SURF CHAMPION OF THE UNIVERSE!

Gulp-gulp-gulp. That was three Dazzy Donuts. (One donut wouldn't be enough for this job!) 'Get underneath me so all our weight is in the same spot,' I yelled at Cat. He flicked me a startled look, but at least he did what I said. Maybe my board was just a badly dinged plank, but Dazzy Donut Dog could do anything. I cross-stepped, slipped into a tail slide off a small wave, carved a bottom turn and a moment later I'd pulled a fakie and we were whizzing backwards. Even the cows we passed were impressed.

'Yee-hah!' I woofed.

'What are you doing?' asked Cat as the board slammed through the waves. At that moment we were caught in an eddy, swirled round and round again. We hurtled towards the far bank and were in danger of crashing at top speed so I attempted a cutback and a moment later it was wipe-out. I opened my eyes underwater and saw Cat spinning round and down. I managed to grab him by a leg and after some pretty desperate doggy paddle, not helped by some very feeble catty paddle, we cast up on a little beach.

We lay there panting, soaked all over again, but I was exploding with excitement.

'Woo-hoo! We almost got mullered!' I yelled at Cat. 'But we made it! Did you see that fakie I did? Oh boy, I am SO stoked!'

Cat shook his soggy head. 'You've swallowed too much river water. I can't understand a

word you're saying. Mullered? Fakie? Stoked? What are you on about?'

'Surf talk, man! It's surf talk. I thought cats knew everything.'

'They know everything worth knowing,' he said evenly, before closing his eyes and going to sleep.

I smiled to myself. I wish Trevor had seen me. He knows everything about surfing and he tells me when we're out walking. I wish he'd seen, and my pups too. Dazzy Donut Dog had definitely saved the day, not to mention saving Cat's life. Twice. And was he grateful? No. Next time I think I might just push him under.

11 More Monsters

We were worn out after the excitement and danger of the river ride. I kept trying to tell Cat how amazing it had been, but he didn't understand.

'All right, so you're good at slurping . . .' he began.

'Surfing,' I barked.

'Whatever. Will you please stop going on about it? Anyone would think it was special.'

'It was special. It saved your life.'

'Brag, brag, brag. That's all you ever do.'

Well! That was a bit rich, coming from Mr Cats-Can-Do-Everything. I shut up after that. I thought if he was going to be like that then there was no point in talking to him – Mr Cool-as-a-Cucumber. Actually, he was more like Mr Boring-as-a-Banana.

'You're sulking,' Cat said, after ten minutes of silence between us.

'Am not,' I said, sounding so sulky I wanted to kick myself.

Cat snorted. That's about as close to laughing as he gets. We bedded down in a wood and we slept like logs – which is just the way you should sleep if you're in a wood.

When we woke we were pretty hungry and guess what? There was nothing to eat. I was getting fed up with this never-any-food business. It was no fun at all. I showed Cat my ribs.

'Look. I'm starving. You'll be able to see right through me soon.'

'We'd better head for a town. We're bound to find something lying around.'

'Good idea, but we'd better be careful. Towns have dog wardens and dog wardens don't like stray dogs. I've had some nasty experiences with dog wardens.'

'You're not a stray. You're only lost. I'm the stray,' Cat said.

'I know that, but the dog wardens don't. Besides, the dog warden in Trevor-Town has got it in for me. She'll bang me up inside.'

'Bang me up inside?' repeated Cat. 'What does that mean? You're talking rubbish again.'

'It means put me in doggy prison. Don't you watch any television at all?'

'No. I have better things to do with my time. Television is for two-legs who don't get out enough and need to fill their brains with fluff.'

Cat was winding me up. I think he does it deliberately. That's what cats are like. Luckily we didn't have a chance to quarrel because at that moment we rounded a corner and there, standing right in front of us was a **HORRIBLE HORROR THING** with a bright red and blue nose, wild eyes and four very hairy arms.

We all screamed, including the Horrible Horror Thing – 'AAARGH!' – and we ran away in three different directions. Then we

turned round and stared at each other. Cat did
a belly crawl across to me. His fur stuck up like
hedgehog quills.

'What is it?' he hissed at me.

'Don't know.'

'It looks like a gorilla with make-up.' Cat
shuddered. 'Where did it come from?'

'Don't know.' I looked at the Horrible
Horror Thing again. It didn't have four hairy
arms. Two of the arms were really legs. It
was just that the two arms it did have were
awfully long. And Cat was right. It *did* look like a
gorilla with make-up. Now it had two large paws
clamped over its eyes. It slowly parted the fingers
on one paw and looked at us with one eye.

'Don't eat me,' it whimpered. Then all of
a sudden it threw both arms wide, leaped
in the air, stuck out its tongue and went
'SPLLLLLURRRGH!'

Cat and I fled.

'Hey!' it shouted after us cheerfully. 'Come

back. Just joking!'

We skidded to a halt and looked back. Horrible Horror Thing was trotting after us. Now I could see it had a long tall tail, whisking in the air. It stopped just short of us, sat down, picked up a stone, threw it casually at a fence and then picked its nose with a bit of twig.

'Hi! Hoolie. That's me. Hoolie Baboon – and not any old kind of baboon either. I'm a mandrill.'

'Really,' muttered Cat. I could tell he wasn't impressed.

'Yes. Mandrills are the bestest kind of baboon
in the baboonery world.' Hoolie was now
cleaning his left ear with the twig. I wish I could
do that.

'Why?' asked Cat.

Hoolie seemed very surprised by this. 'Why?
Why?' he repeated several times. 'We just are.
The best. Definitely. Cos I said.' Hoolie glanced
round. 'Seen any windscreen wipers lately?'

Cat and I exchanged looks again. Windscreen
wipers? What was he on about? I shook my head.

'Shame. They're good fun. Never mind.
There's always another day, as my granny used to
say. Though actually she didn't, cos I didn't have
a granny, but I bet she would have said things like
that, if I'd had one, cos grannies do.'

'Are you always like this?' Cat asked.

'Like what?'

'Bonkers,' Cat said starkly.

Hoolie grinned at us, beat his chest with both
fists, lifted his head and began to chant, getting
louder and higher all the time.

'Hoo-hoo-hoo-HOO-HOO-HOO-
HOOLIE-BOO!' he yelled, and did a back
flip. His head suddenly darted forward and
he fixed Cat with one eye. 'Bonkers?' he
repeated. 'No way!'

I think Hoolie eats
special donuts.

12 Bad Behaviour

Hoolie's wild grin slowly froze on his face.
His eyes darted from one side to the other. He
shuffled forward and whispered, 'Have you seen
. . . THE THING?'

'What thing?' I asked.

'THE THING,' repeated Hoolie. 'Glowing
eyes and slashing claws. It tried to bite my b-b-b–'

'Back?' I suggested.

'No – my BUM!'

Hoolie whirled round to show his rear end.
I had a sniff. Definitely not at all doggy, but it
did remind me of that strange scent near the
shopping centre.

'The Thing wanted a bum sandwich,' cried
Hoolie. 'But I leaped out of the way and it ate

my neighbour instead and I escaped.'

'The Beast,' I muttered, and Cat nodded.

'No, no. It wasn't The Beast. It was The Thing.'

'Same thing,' murmured Cat. 'So where did you escape from?'

'Safari Park. We were attacked by The Thing. Horrible. Slish-slash, blood, bodies, nightmare.' It might seem odd, but all the time Hoolie was telling us this awful story he was trying to stand on his head, and repeatedly falling over.

'So, where are we going?' asked Hoolie, making his fifth attempt at a headstand.

'Streaker and I are going home to her house,' announced Cat stiffly.

'I've got three pups,' I announced. 'And they are the cutest things ever. One's got a teeny-tiny pink tongue that sticks out all the time, and one wags his tail so fast it's just a blur, and the other has —'

'I'm coming with you,' announced Hoolie cheerfully as he crumpled into a heap yet again.

'OK,' I said.

'OK?' hissed Cat. 'OK? You want a bonkers baboon to come with us?'

'Yes. Why not?'

'Give me one good reason,' Cat demanded.

'Safety in numbers.'

'Yes,' Hoolie butted in and he banged his chest with pride. 'And I am an expert in ba-ba-ba-boom.'

'Ba-ba-ba-boom?' Cat echoed.

'The ancient baboon art of fighting without getting hurt.'

'I know I shall kick myself for asking this question,' said Cat. 'But how does that work?'

'We make a loud noise like this – BA-BA-BA-BOOM! And then we run away as fast as we can before they get over their surprise.'

But Cat and I had already flung ourselves under a bush to escape his wild yell.

'See?' said Hoolie, triumphantly. 'It works best

BA-BA-BA-BOOM!

if you fling your arms about a lot at the same time. It's pretty wild.'

Cat shook his head in disbelief. Finally he beamed a wide, false smile at Hoolie and said: 'You are most welcome to join our wonderful little party. Please feel free to snack upon the tasty morsels we don't have and share in the delight of our journey to nowhere in particular.'

'Ignore him,' I advised the baboon.

So we continued our trek and Hoolie didn't stop yackety-yacking the whole time. I thought his jaw would fall off, he opened and shut it so often. Blah blah blah blah blah blah. He didn't stop until we reached the edge of a town and he saw a row of parked cars outside a fish and chip shop.

Hoolie stopped dead in his tracks. His mouth fell open and stayed that way until drool began dribbling over his fat, hairy, red lips. His eyes glazed over and he began to mutter to himself.

'Boing! Twang! Ping! Poyoing! I am in baboon

heaven.' Suddenly he took off, at top speed, bounding down the road until he hurled himself straight on top of the first car.

Before we could stop him he was bouncing on the roofs, ripping off aerials, wrenching off the windscreen wipers and battering the side mirrors until they fell off or just dangled uselessly at the side.

Cat and I hurried over. 'What are you

DOING?'

'Boingy, twangy things!' yelled Hoolie with delight. 'Look!' He twanged an aerial so hard it snapped in two. Then he grabbed a mirror, put his feet against the side of the car and pulled it off – GRRRRRANNGGG! – just like that. He stared into it for a second, tossed it over one shoulder and as it landed made a big explosive noise. 'BOOOOOM! Bombs away!'

At that moment several people came out of the fish and chip shop. They took one look at us and came steaming towards us, shouting furiously.

'Uh-oh!' said Hoolie. 'Time for some ba-ba-ba-boom!'

He began jumping up and down on the car roof, screeching and yelling and waving his extra-long arms like some hairy windmill gone mad. Then he ran STRAIGHT TOWARDS THEM!!! Cat and I were amazed to see the crowd freeze in terror, while Hoolie went straight up to the nearest two-legs, grabbed her fish and chips and

came hurtling back towards us, grinning like a
maniac, dashed past us and on up the street.

'Run for it!' he yelled over his shoulder at us.
So we did. Soon the noisy crowd was far behind.
We found a quiet place in the park. Hoolie
spread out the fish and chips on the newspaper
wrapping.

'Grub,' he said, and we all tucked in. Cat was

being very quiet. He usually talked a lot, mostly about himself. But ever since we had met Hoolie he had hardly said anything. Now he sat back, licked his lips, washed his paws and ears and began.

'Please tell me what you were doing back there. I have never seen anything like that in all my life.'

'Really?' Hoolie was surprised too. 'That's what we do in the Safari Park. We jump on cars and pull their twangy bits. It's brilliant. The two-legs don't like it, you know. It makes them cross.'

'But why do it at all?' I asked.

Hoolie shrugged. 'Isn't it obvious? We're building our own.'

'You're building your own cars?' Cat repeated.

'Yeah! Only most times we don't get all the right bits, so we keep having to get more. We've got loads and loads of aerials and stuff. But we're short on seats and engines and steering wheels and so on.'

'Can you drive?' I asked.

Hoolie burst out laughing. 'Don't be daft! We don't want to drive them. We just want to pull off their aerials in the winter when there aren't any visitors. We get bored. Very bored.'

Cat rolled his eyes. 'This is your fault,' he told me. 'You said he should come with us. Now we have a lunatic on board.'

'He got us out of that mess with those angry people just now,' I pointed out.

'He got us INTO that mess with those angry people,' growled Cat. 'It was because of him they were angry!'

'And he got us those very nice fish and chips,' I added. Cat fell silent. He sat back and glared hard at both of us. He does it so well – glaring. Until he fell asleep of course, but by that time Hoolie and I were asleep too.

13 Red Bottom Dog

I woke before Hoolie, but Cat was already awake
and staring at a photo in the greasy newspaper
left over from the fish and chips.

ESCAPED CHEETAH
STILL ON LOOSE
The Cheetah that escaped from

'That's a very big cat,' I said, and Cat nodded
slowly.

'It's a distant cousin of mine, from Africa.'

'Really? Why is it in the newspaper?' I asked. We both gazed at the article beneath the photograph.

ESCAPED CHEETAH
STILL ON LOOSE

The cheetah that escaped from Trapham Safari Park five days ago is still on the loose. Park officials say the animal killed several baboons in the park. Two baboons escaped from the park at the same time. One has been recaptured but the other is still at large. Safari Park officials have advised anyone in the area to keep their pets indoors until both animals have been caught.

'What does it say?' I asked Cat.

'Not much,' he said. 'It says cheetahs are the fastest land animals known to Man.'

'They haven't seen me!' I cried.

Cat almost spat. 'There is no way you could beat a cheetah. Look at those legs! Look at the body! That cousin of mine is a speed-machine. Now look at you! You're a fat, bow-legged dog with bad breath.'

I ignored him. 'What else does the newspaper say? There must be more.'

Cat sighed and ran a paw along each line of print as he read it.

'It says cheetahs have nicer fur than dogs and can run much faster than dogs and they can climb trees, which dogs can't do, and they have much better eyesight than dogs, and bigger brains too.'

I sat back. I thought it was a strange article to put in a newspaper but Cat said that was what the newspaper said, so it must be true.

'He's my cousin,' Cat went on, 'which explains why I have a big brain.'

'Baboons have bigger brains than cats,' yawned Hoolie, as he stirred.

'Oh?'

'Yes, because really we are just like two-legs only we are stronger and better looking. Look at them! The only fur they have left is that tiny bit stuck on top of their heads like a little tufty-wufty thing. Apart from that they're all bare! Yuk! And I bet they can't make their bottoms go bright red.'

'You can't do that!' I exploded.

'Can. Well, not me, but some of us can. I've seen it. Bright-red bottoms, lots of them. I bet you can't do that.'

I went into a corner to think. What a strange world I was in. I looked at Hoolie, with his bright red and blue nose. I thought about having a red bottom. Then I thought about having an orange bottom like the cross two-legs, but a red bottom sounded so cool. I could be the only dog in the world with a red bum. I think Red Bottom Dog would be even better than Dazzy Donut Dog. In fact Dazzy Donut Dog sounded pretty stupid really. Yeah, from now on I would be Red Bottom Dog!

I thought about my pups too and wondered how they were getting on. I was sure Trevor was looking after them but he's not their mum, is he? I should be there, teaching them how to sniff each other and lick things and jump on chairs and chew pillows and all that doggy stuff. I missed them worse than ever.

'Tomorrow,' I told the other two, 'we are going home.'

'Africa, here I come!' yelled Hoolie.

'Not Africa, Hoolie. My home, where my pups are, and Trevor.'

'Trevor?' asked the baboon.

'He's a baby two-legs,' snapped Cat in disgust.

'Has he got a car?' asked Hoolie dreamily.

Cat turned back to me. 'How are we going to get home? Do you suddenly know the way?'

I shook my head and my ears flapped. I felt good about this. Flapping ears always makes me feel good. 'I feel it in my bones. Trust me. Tomorrow we will find home. I'm sure of it. What we need now is a good place to sleep.'

Well, that's what I said – we needed a good place to sleep. Do you know what we did? We all slept up a tree. We did. Even me! I know dogs can't climb trees, but I'm Red Bottom Dog now and Red Bottom Dog can do anything. Mind you, Cat and Hoolie did help pull me up.

'Why are we doing this?' I asked them.

'Oh, you know . . .' began Cat, and trailed off.

'No, I don't know. That's why I'm asking.'

'In case, you know . . .' started Hoolie, but didn't finish.

Then I realized. They were scared. We were all scared. We were being relentlessly tracked down by a dark Beast of the Night. Every night it seemed to come that little bit closer. I hastily scrambled up the tree.

It's a bit weird, sleeping up a tree. I don't know how cats and baboons manage, I really don't. It wasn't long before Hoolie was snoring away like one of those road drill thingies that go *Gurr Gurr Gurr GRRRRRR! Gurr Gurr Gurr GRRRRR!* Cat's whiskers were twitching away too, which means he was off in Dreamland, but I was WIDE AWAKE.

How do you sleep on a branch? You can't! It's stupid. Who'd want to sleep up there? Cat and Hoolie said it was safer but I think that really really really they were hoping I'd fall off. And guess what? I did. Even though I was wide awake and clinging on with my paws and my

tail and my ears and my tongue and all my fur
– everything was locked on to that branch – I fell
off, WHEE! BANG! OW! PAIN!

That woke the others up and serves them right
too. Fancy going off to Dreamland while I fall
out of a tree. They helped me back up and we
were just settling back to sleep when . . .

WE SAW THE BEAST! WE SAW THE THING! WE ALMOST DIED!

14 Homeward Bound

First of all it was just an almost-noise. It went
like this: - I put all
those little lines there because it was like the noise
of silent walking and I think that line looks like
silent footsteps, don't you? You have to imagine
them going pad pad pad pad, along the ground
like that, only silently. That's why I called it an
almost-noise.

I think we must have heard it in our inner
brain. Except of course Hoolie hasn't got an
inner brain because he's a baboon and they
don't use their brains. I know that's true, because
if they did they wouldn't go round making car
aerials go TWANG!

We sat up in the tree, dead still, and with me

holding on with my tongue and tail and legs
and everything. I could feel myself slip-slipping,
sliding off the branch – AND THEN IT CAME
OUT OF THE SHADOWS!

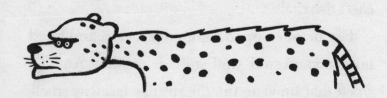

It was that thing in the newspaper! It went slinking along right under our tree and THEN IT STOPPED! RIGHT BENEATH ME! AND I WAS SLIP-SLIDING! Hoolie held on to my ears and Cat tried to stop my bum sliding off the branch and I thought: *We are all going to DIE!*

I wondered what Red Bottom Dog would do and I knew she wouldn't be scared, so I pretended I wasn't, even though I was. I pretended I wasn't quivering with fear, even though I was. And I pretended I wasn't slipping off the branch, even though I was. And I pretended Hoolie was holding my ears to be helpful and not because he thought they might be as much fun as windscreen wipers, which I'm sure he was definitely thinking, because he's mad and trying to build a car and he's a baboon that can't drive.

The Beast stopped right underneath and lifted his head and sniff sniff sniffed, like that. And I smelt that smell again, the strange faraway smell and now I knew what it was. It was the smell of long grass, hot sun and great herds of antelope, and the cheetah creep-creeping up on them, with his long swishing tail and sharp teeth.

Now his yellow eyes narrowed and he looked all around. And then he did a great big wee all over the tree trunk! He did! Honestly! He growled quietly, a low rumble – *rrrrrrrrrrrrrr*. After that he did a bit more sniffing and then he went off again, like this: - - - - - - - - - - - - - - - - (More silent padding.)

And we were still up the tree and we'd been holding our breath for days! So we had to let it out and take a big, deep breath. Phew! We had seen THE BEAST and we had survived. Red Bottom Dog saved the day! Then Hoolie let go of my ears and I fell out of the tree again. CRASH! OW! MORE PAIN!

As I lay on the ground I thought: *Actually, come to think of it, Red Bottom Dog wasn't much use up that tree at all.* I'm going to stick with Dazzy Donut

Dog after all. I think donuts are much better than red bottoms, don't you?

Hoolie asked if we'd noticed The Beast had two tails.

Cat said its teeth were like daggers.

I said my ears hurt, and gave Hoolie a sharp look, but he just grinned.

We set off and found a road. I was really pleased because, although I hadn't told anyone, I had a secret plan. I'd been thinking about it for some time. This is how my plan went. *We find a van with the back doors open. We get inside. It takes us back to where I came from.* Wasn't that a good idea? I thought it was, and you know what? We saw a van, with the doors open. It was parked outside a house. And another thing – when I looked inside, it was full of pies and sausage rolls! In fact, it was the same van, because I could smell where I'd been sick.

'I was sick in here!' I told the others. 'Jump in!'

'I'm not sitting where you threw up,' Cat

complained.

'Just get in,' I said.

Hoolie didn't mind where he sat. He was far too busy admiring himself in the wing mirror he'd just pulled off the side. Then he found the pies and began to eat one.

'Don't eat too much, or you'll be sick like I was,' I warned.

'Oh, pishy-poo to you!' he chomped, cramming another pie into his mouth.

We hid behind some boxes and soon the driver came along, and it was the same one – the one with the dark glasses – and he shut the door and off we went.

We hadn't gone very far before Hoolie said
he didn't feel well. Cat said it was because he'd
been looking at himself in the mirror for too
long. Hoolie made a grab for Cat's tail but wasn't
nearly quick enough.

'Stop it, the pair of you,' I snapped. 'We're
almost home.' Amazingly, they both shut up and
Hoolie wasn't sick either.

'When the van stops, wait for my order,' I said.
I could smell home. I was sure we were heading
in the right direction. I could almost hear my
puppies calling to me. *Hey, Mum! We're here! Come
on, hurry up! We've missed you so much!*

The van slowed and stopped. The driver got
out. He began to open the doors.

'Run for it! Ba-ba-ba-boom!' I yelled.

We bounded out of the back of the van,
knocking the man flying, with Hoolie still
clutching a haul of stolen pies. He was a pie
thief! My puppies were practically shouting to me
now. All I had to do was find out exactly where

I was. And guess where we were? Right in the middle of Trevor-Town, in the market place.

'I know where I am!' I told the others happily. 'We'll be home in zippity-zip.'

Cat and Hoolie were standing back to back – the defensive position – looking round the market. 'Why is it so quiet? Where are all the two-legs?' asked Cat suspiciously.

It was true. There was nobody to be seen. Strange. Eerie. Sinister. A cold feeling began to creep right over me, making my fur stand on end.

AND THEN WE SAW THE BEAST!

In broad daylight! It was a cheetah – the fastest land animal known to Man, and it was stalking towards us. Cat went yowling up a telephone pole, closely followed by Hoolie. That just left me, on my own. And I can't climb telephone poles.

I was transfixed. The cheetah's glowing eyes were fixed on me. I WAS THE TARGET! My tail went between my back legs. My ears went right back, my lip curled and I felt so scared and fierce at the same time and I thought I was going to die.

Cat sat right on top of the telephone pole, hissing and spitting. Hoolie sat just below Cat hurling pies down at the cheetah and screaming at me. 'Go get him, Streaker! Biff his nose! Stamp on his toes! Pull his tail! Poke him in the eye!'

I wished he would shut up.

There was no escape. What would Dazzy Donut Dog do? This was a mega-emergency. It was going to need at least six extra-special-super-dooper-nuclear-power-plus-iced Dazzy Donuts with multi-coloured sprinkly bits AND jam, but Dazzy Donut Dog was TOO SCARED TO EAT THEM!

The only thing that could save me now was – ME!

15 Who's the Fastest? Guess Who!

The cheetah paused. It crouched. Its body arched like a coiled spring. It waggled its bottom briefly and then WHOOOOOOOSH! It came at me like a rocket with teeth.

My brain jangled into activity. I thought: *I am not Red Bottom Dog and I am not Dazzy Donut Dog – I am Streaker, the fastest dog in the world and now I am going to run even faster than a cheetah or I am going to die!* And guess what? I did!

I ran like an even bigger rocket than the cheetah and he was right on my heels and we twisted and turned and he almost got me and he almost didn't and sometimes I fell over my own feet and sometimes he fell over his feet and I could hear him going *pant pant pant* right on my

tail and my ears were streaming out behind me
like twin jet trails.

All the time the cheetah was snapping at me
with his teeth going *snip! snap!* but he kept missing
and I ran ran ran ran ran until I thought my legs
would fly off my body or they'd get worn right

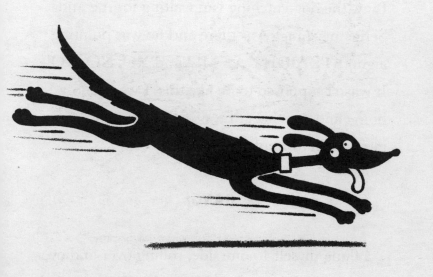

down to teeny-tiny stumps or just maybe they'd
turn into wings and I would take off into the sky
and fly to safety!

I went racing round a corner and suddenly I
was RUNNING DOWN TREVOR'S ROAD
STRAIGHT TOWARDS THE HOUSE AND –

NO, NO! THE ROAD WAS BLOCKED!

There were loads of policemen in the way and I saw the dog-catching van waiting for me and Sergeant Smugg was there and he was pointing a gun STRAIGHT AT ME! and NO, NO, NO! It wasn't supposed to be like this! I was almost home and the cheetah was behind me and the gun was in front of me and

BANG!

I flung myself to one side, rolling over and over and over in the dust and I thought: *This really isn't fair. I've outrun the fastest animal known to Man, and now I've been shot dead! That's not fair at all!* Then I thought: *Hang on, my brain is still thinking, so I can't be dead.*

I got up and looked around and the cheetah was lying on its side. It was breathing, but it was

asleep, because Sergeant Smugg hadn't shot me, he had stuck the cheetah with a special dart kind of thing that made it go to Dreamland – zzzzzz.

Do you know what all those two-legs did after that? They ignored me! I had run faster than the fastest animal on earth, and all the two-legs could do was go and look at some big spotty cat. I ask you!

I crept away and Hoolie and Cat came and found me and we went sneaking past the dog warden's van just in case. My heart was beating faster and faster but I wasn't scared any more, I was bursting with woofy happiness because now I was trotting up my very own front path and standing at the door to my very own Trevor's house.

'WOOF! WOOF! WOOF! OPEN THIS DOOR AT ONCE! WOOF! WOOF! I WANT TO SEE MY PUPPIES!'

Do you know something? Nothing happened! I took a step back.

'They didn't hear you,' suggested Hoolie. 'Shall I throw a brick through the window?'

'NO! Leave it to me,' I snapped. Honestly, baboons — you can't take them anywhere. I barked again.

'WOOF! WOOF! WOOF! LET ME IN!
I MUST SEE MY PUPPIES!'

And guess what? The door opened and out
they came! All three of them, bounce-bounce-
bounce, lick-lick-lick, love-love-love, and we
rolled about and they bit me and I pretended to
spank them with my paw, only very, very gently
and we hugged and bounced and licked all over
again. Then we sniffed each other's bottoms,
because that's the best way to say 'Hello!'

Trevor sat on the front doorstep watching and
he was crying! He was! The big booby! Then his
mum and dad came out and they frowned and I
could see they were frowning at Cat and Hoolie.
They weren't at all happy about that, but Trevor
said they ought to stay. Mrs Two-Legs said she
was definitely not having a cat in the house and
Mr Two-Legs told Hoolie to get off his car and
put the aerial back and what did a baboon need
windscreen wipers for anyway? Then he went
inside to ring the Safari Park to tell them there

was a mad baboon in his front garden and would they please come and remove it immediately, and they did, because they were only just up the road, waiting with the dog warden's van. It wasn't there for me – it was for Hoolie and the cheetah!

Cat curled between Mrs Two-Legs's feet and purred and rubbed against her and jumped up into her arms and nuzzled her and purred and of course she gave in and said how nice he was.

'You are so sweet,' she drooled. 'And I'm going to call you Cutie-pops.'

Cat glanced back at me and told me to wipe the grin off my face.

So that was how I got lost and found (twice!) and had an adventure and outran a cheetah and my puppies are brilliant and if you turn over the page you can see a special picture of me and them. Oh yes, and I don't bother to be Dazzy Donut Dog any more because actually I think I am quite enough of a super-dog without having to pretend. But I do still like donuts.

And last of all, you know what? Cat has been teaching me some more reading and writing and I have written a story for you.

GQ SSSSSSZZZZZZ O

It's brilliant isn't it? Maybe you can't read yet, so I'll tell you what it says.

I am the fastest dog in the world.

That G thing is the cheetah with his mouth open going *pant pant pant*, and the Q mark is obviously me with my tail of course.

SSSSSSZZZZZZ is me running really fast fast fast, and twisting and turning.

The round O thing is the world. Cat said *No it isn't, it's an orange*, and we had an argument. I said it can't be an orange or my story would say *I am the fastest dog in the orange*, and that was stupid and I told him to stop arguing or I'd bite his tail again, so he stopped, though he mutters 'orange' under his breath sometimes when he thinks I'm not listening but I am. Anyhow, O is the world, so that's what my story says:

I am the fastest dog in the world.

And I am too!

With regard to the unfortunate incident on page 23, Streaker would like to point out that not all female dogs can do that, but she can because she's clever, so there!